Christmas comes to Mrs Mouse
by
PEGGY BURTON

© THE MEDICI SOCIETY LTD · LONDON 1985.   Printed in England. B83   ISBN 0 85503 083 6

It was the morning of Christmas Eve and Mr Rabbit was getting ready to go out in his shiny new car. It was a holly-berry red and he kept it in a shelter he had made in the roots of an old oak tree close to where he lived with Mrs Rabbit and their two children, Ben and Betsy.

He was going to fetch Matilda Mouse whom they had invited to spend Christmas with them because she lived all by herself and they thought she would be lonely.

'Can I come with you?' asked Ben. 'You can all come if you like,' said his father; 'but don't forget to wrap up warmly.' There was great excitement; Mrs Rabbit packed a basket with hot drinks and biscuits.

Ben and Betsy scampered out to the car feeling cosy in their warm coats and bright woolly scarves. 'I'd like to stop on the way at the village store, because there are several things I need for to-morrow,' said Mrs Rabbit as she got into the car.

'Certainly,' said Mr Rabbit.

They took rugs in case it should get any colder and a spade in case it snowed. 'Hop in!' said Mr Rabbit to the two bunnies; then he settled himself in the driving seat, started the engine, and they were off.

As it was a lovely crisp sunny morning Mr Rabbit had put the hood down and they waved to their friends the squirrels as they drove along, and Robin Redbreast flew out to see them. As they passed Mr Badger, who was outside his house cutting logs, he called out 'Do you think we'll have snow for Christmas?' 'I hope so,' yelled Ben. 'But not before we get back home, thank you,' said Mr Rabbit.

Before very long they arrived at Mrs Prickles' Store and Mrs Rabbit and Betsy went in and bought some fruit and nuts and vegetables and exciting goodies for the next day.

Mr Rabbit and Ben, outside in the car, heard a Tweet! Tweet! 'Hello Robin!' said Ben; for there standing on the bonnet was Robin Redbreast who had flown after them for fun to see if he could keep up with the car.

Just as Mrs Rabbit and Betsy came out with their shopping, a mouse rode up on a bicycle; he wished them a happy Christmas and dashed into the shop.

'Good Morning!' said Mrs Prickles from behind the counter, 'And how is Mrs Mouse today?' 'Not very well,' said the mouse, 'but I'm sure that a bottle of your special honey cough-cure is what she needs.'

Then Mr Mouse bought one or two things which his wife had asked him to get. 'And how are you managing for Christmas?' said Mrs Prickles. 'I'm afraid it will be very dull for the children,' said Mr Mouse, 'because we haven't been able to get things ready.' 'Tell Mrs Mouse this is a present from me,' said Mrs Prickles as she put a Christmas pudding into the bag.

'You are very kind,' said Mr Mouse. Then he wished her a happy Christmas and went outside and put everything in his bicycle basket. 'Don't forget your change,' called Mrs Prickles. Mr Mouse ran back into the shop, thanked her again but when he got outside his bike had gone.

'Come back!' he shouted as he looked along the road and saw Sammy Shrew riding away on his bike. 'Help! Help!' he squealed (as naughty Sammy pedalled faster and faster and was now almost out of sight). 'Stop him, somebody.'

Robin Redbreast heard him and quickly flew up over the trees and across the fields and lots of other birds, wondering what all the noise was about, flew along beside him.

When naughty Sammy came round a bend in the road he suddenly saw all the birds flying straight at him. He was so frightened that he started to wobble all over the road and finally toppled over the handlebars onto his nose.

'That will teach you a lesson,' said Robin as Sammy ran away across the field, rubbing his sore nose as he went. When he had disappeared Robin thanked the other birds for their help, and flew back to tell Mr Mouse where his bike was. 'I'm afraid it's quite a long way off,' he said, 'but I'll come with you and show you where it is.'

While Mr Mouse was trudging along the road to rescue his bike, Mr Rabbit and his family had reached a corner in the lane where a signpost read – 'Matilda Mouse lives along here'. Mr Rabbit manoeuvred his car carefully along a narrow lane and there in a hollow was a quaint little house and Matilda was standing at the window waiting for them.

Ben and Betsy went to help with Matilda's luggage while she followed behind with her arms full of presents all wrapped in Christmassy paper. Mrs Rabbit greeted her with a big hug and said she was so pleased to see her.

Before they settled Matilda on the back seat between the two bunnies, Mr Rabbit put up the hood of the car because a few black clouds were appearing overhead.

As they drove back the clouds increased and little flurries of snow started to fall and by the time they reached the road again it was snowing quite hard. It got heavier and heavier and before very long everything was covered with a thick layer of white until Mr Rabbit found it difficult to see the edge of the road, and just after passing a notice which read – 'Squirrel Nurseries – Christmas Trees For Sale' – the car skidded and with a bump the front wheels went into a ditch.

MATILDA MOUSE
LIVES ALONG
HERE

'I'm afraid you'll all have to get out,' said Mr Rabbit. But this was rather difficult because the car was leaning at an angle and Matilda had slipped down and almost disappeared under her rug. The bunnies wriggled out and finally they managed to rescue Matilda.

'Now,' said Mr Rabbit, 'If we all push perhaps we can get back on to the road.' The two young ones clambered down into the ditch and everybody pushed and pushed, but the car wouldn't move.

Then Mr Rabbit took the spade out of the boot and tried to dig the snow away but by now it was snowing so hard that he couldn't work fast enough and as he threw a shovelful of snow over his shoulder a squeaky little voice called out – 'Please stop Mister! You're covering up our front door.' And when Mr Rabbit turned round a little mouse popped his head out of the snow.

'Well! Well! Well!' said Mr Rabbit, 'And who might you be?'

'I'm Timothy Mouse' was the reply, 'and you're blocking our doorway and please we need some help. Our mother isn't well and our father went off early this morning on his bike to get some medicine, and we think something has gone wrong because he hasn't come back yet.'

'Show me where your mother is,' said Mrs Rabbit, 'and we'll see what we can do to help.' Ben and Timothy moved some of the snow away from a little door under the tree and when they had all squeezed through, they found themselves in quite a large room and there was poor Mrs Mouse sitting in a chair wrapped in blankets with two baby mice beside her. She was so pleased to see them.

Mrs Rabbit sent Ben to get the basket from the car while she explained to Mrs Mouse how they were stuck in the ditch. Mrs Mouse felt a little better after she was given a hot drink, and said, 'There is an empty house next to ours where Mr Badger used to live and you could all shelter there until the snow stops and you get your car back on the road.' Then Matilda said, 'If you would like to go to see the house, I'll stay behind and look after Mrs Mouse and the twins.'

Mr Rabbit thought it was just what they needed and he asked Ben and Betsy to bring in all the things from the car while he borrowed a lantern from Timothy and went in search of Mr Mouse.

He had been walking a long time in the direction of the shop and it was getting quite dark. He stopped and listened but there wasn't a sound. He lit the lantern and a soft yellow glow lit his path in the snow.

As he trudged along he kept calling, 'Mister Mouse! . . . *Mister Mouse!*' and all at once he heard a squeaky little singing voice coming towards him, and into the light of his lantern came Mr Mouse struggling along with his shopping bag.

'Hello there!' said Mr Rabbit. 'Aren't you the little man I saw at the shop? What's happened to your bike?' 'A naughty shrew went off with it, and when I found it the front wheel was buckled, so I had to push it back to the shop and leave it with Mrs Prickles,' said Mr Mouse, 'and tell me, what are *you* doing here?'

'I came to search for you,' said Mr Rabbit, 'because everybody was getting worried about you.'

Then he told Mr Mouse all that had been going on and asked him how he would manage for Christmas Day.

'It won't be very merry', said Mr Mouse, 'because, although my wife is nearly well again, we haven't been able to get things prepared.' They trudged along with Mr Rabbit carrying the shopping bag and when they at last reached home and knocked on the door young Timothy rushed to open it and shouted, 'They're here! It's Pa! He's home!' Everybody was so excited to see them back safely and Mr Mouse said he wouldn't have been able to get there without Mr Rabbit's help.

Later that evening Mr Rabbit told his wife and Matilda what Mr Mouse had said about Christmas Day. So they decided there and then that they would all work to give the Mouse family a happy Christmas.

Mrs Rabbit and Betsy opened the bags of shopping and made a lovely Christmas cake and Mr Rabbit and Ben went out with the lantern to buy a Christmas tree from Squirrel Nurseries, while Matilda looked through all her parcels to see how many presents she had. They all worked to get everything ready and went to bed feeling very happy at the thought of the next day.

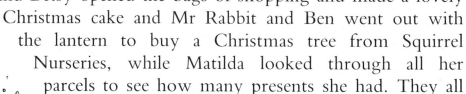

Ben Bunny woke on Christmas morning wondering where he was. Then he remembered what they had done the night before.

He got out of bed quietly and crept into the big room where everything was as they had left it. The table had been set, and in the middle was the lovely big Christmas cake. In a corner of the room stood the Christmas tree which Matilda had decorated with all the little presents she had been making during the year. They were all wrapped in shiny coloured paper and tied with bright ribbon. Then Betsy had added the tinsel and the baubles she had bought at Mrs Prickles' Store.

Ben thought it all looked wonderful and it wasn't long before he had everybody awake and out of bed. They all went next door and found that Mrs Mouse was feeling much better.

'Will you all come and spend the day with us?' said Mrs Rabbit. 'We'd love to have you and we seem to have everything we need, except a Christmas pudding.' 'That's soon put right; Mrs Prickles sent me one as a present,' said Mrs Mouse and she thanked Mrs Rabbit for the invitation.

They all went in to Badger's old house and Mrs Mouse was amazed when she saw what had been done.

23

Oh, what a feast they had and what a wonderful day.

The children played games together and Matilda managed to find a present for each one of them.

At the end of the day Timothy opened the door and cried 'Look! The snow has stopped and the stars have come out.' Everyone ran to see.

'This is the merriest Christmas ever,' sighed Mrs Mouse and everybody agreed.